Treasure Island

Retold by
Stewart Ross

Illustrated by
Alex Paterson

ARCTURUS

For Ana Ross, with much love—SR.

For Martha and Molly—AP.

ARCTURUS

This edition published in 2018 by Arcturus Publishing Limited
26/27 Bickels Yard, 151–153 Bermondsey Street,
London SE1 3HA

Writer: Stewart Ross
Illustrator: Alex Paterson
Designer: Jeni Child
Editor: Sebastian Rydberg
Art Director: Jessica Crass

ISBN: 978-1-78828-695-4
CH006096NT
Supplier 24, Date 0318, Print run 6737

Printed in Malaysia

ways horrified me. Mother and Father weren't too pleased, either. But he paid in gold, and we needed the money.

Every day, the old rogue kept a lookout on the clifftops. In the evenings, when he had drunk too much rum, he laid his cutlass before him on the table and sang an old sea song in a high, salty voice:

Fifteen men on the dead man's chest—
Yo-ho-ho, and a bottle of rum!

Captain Bones walked the cliffs to watch for a "seafaring man with one leg." He was obviously terrified of this one-legged sailor, and every month promised me a silver four-penny coin, if I kept an eye open for him. I did so, but he never paid me the money.

One day, the Captain had a visitor, a pale, scrawny sailor with two fingers missing from his left hand. "Black Dog!" the Captain gasped when he saw him.

For a while, the two men sat drinking rum and chatting. Gradually, their talk became angry, and they swore loudly at each other. When Black Dog asked a question, and the Captain shouted "No! No!" they began to fight.

Cutlasses clashed. The Captain lunged at Black Dog, who screamed and ran for the door. The Captain chased after him.

He aimed a mighty blow at Black Dog's head, but his cutlass hit the inn sign, and the rogue escaped.

The sudden exercise was too much for the Captain, and he collapsed to the floor. His life was saved by Dr. Livesey, who had called to treat my sick father. Nevertheless, the Captain knew that Black Dog would return, and next time he would not be alone.

Dr. Livesey told Captain Bones that if he went on drinking rum he would die. "Billy Bones," as Black Dog had called him, took no notice. After forcing me to bring him a tot of rum, he explained what was happening.

He had been the first mate on Captain Flint's ship. This Flint was one of the most  cruel, greedy, and rich pirates who ever sailed the seas. As he lay dying, he gave Bones a map. It showed where he'd buried his gold and money on Treasure Island.

The crew of Flint's ship knew about the map. They knew Billy Bones had it, too. That's why he was hiding in our inn and keeping a daily watch from the cliffs. He was looking out for the pirates who wanted his precious map of Treasure Island.

Now Black Dog had found him, Bones was terrified. It wasn't Black Dog who scared him—it was the mysterious sailor with one leg.

*

Yes, I was alarmed by these bloodthirsty stories of pirates and treasure. But at the time, I had other things on my mind: shortly after Black Dog's visit, my father died.

Mother and I were now alone—and the murderous pirates were closing in.

The afternoon after my father's funeral, a blind man came tap-tapping along the road to our inn. He wore a huge cape and a hood over his head. When I approached him, he grabbed me with fingers of steel.

"Take me to the Captain!" he ordered.

"I dare not," I replied.

"Do it—or I'll break your arm!" he sneered.

I had to obey. I led the blind man to Billy Bones. When the two of them met, he handed over a piece of paper. That done, he spun round and disappeared up the road.

Bones looked at the paper. "The Black Spot warning!" he groaned. "I have six hours to hand over the map—or else!"

The shock was too much for him. He swayed and fell to the floor. Dead.

Cruel and harsh though Bones had been, I couldn't help crying. When my mother heard the noise and came downstairs, I told her all I knew. I told her about Captain Flint and his buried treasure, about the secret map that Flint had given to Billy Bones, and about the blind man and the Black Spot warning.

"The pirates will be here in six hours!" I cried. "What shall we do?"

Mother and I hurried to the village and begged for help. The people were too frightened to go back with us, but they did send for the police officers.

It was dark when we returned to the Admiral Benbow. Billy Bones hadn't paid us for months, and mother needed the money. We discovered the key of his sea chest and unlocked it. Inside were a bag of coins and a waterproof packet.

As mother counted the coins, a low whistle sounded—the attack signal! "They're coming!" I whispered.

Mother grabbed the coins, I took the packet, and we hurried outside.

We hid under a bridge and listened as the pirates smashed open the inn door and searched the place. They were furious when they realized the map was missing. Shouting and swearing, they ran into the road.

At that moment, the police galloped up, and the pirates scattered into the darkness. While friends looked after mother, I went with the police to find Dr. Livesey. I met him with his friend, Squire Trelawney, and together, we unwrapped the waterproof packet. Inside was a map—the map of Treasure Island.

CHAPTER 2

The *Hispaniola*

Dr. Livesey and Squire Trelawney decided to sail to Treasure Island and take me with them. We would find Captain Flint's buried treasure and be as rich as kings!

The Squire rode to Bristol to buy a ship. A few weeks later, he sent a letter saying he had bought a fine ship, the *Hispaniola*, and got an excellent crew to sail it.

The Squire's letter was exciting, but it worried me. He had told all Bristol about our voyage. What if wicked people—pirates even—heard about our map of Treasure Island? They might try to steal it.

I was also worried about a man the Squire had met. He said he was a brave old sailor who would be our ship's cook. He had helped the Squire choose the *Hispaniola*'s crew, too. His name was Long John Silver—and he had one leg.

Captain Bones had warned me about a "seafaring man with one leg." I hoped Mr. Silver was not him.

The next day, I said goodbye to my mother and set out for Bristol. Squire Trelawney was at the docks to meet me. "We sail tomorrow!" he said.

After breakfast, the Squire gave me a note for Long John Silver. I'd find him at the Spyglass Inn, he said.

I found the inn easily enough— and there stood a "seafaring man with one leg." He was tall and strong, with a smiling face as big as a ham. As  his left leg had been cut off at the hip, he walked very deftly with the help of a crutch.

On his shoulder sat a green-and-red parrot.

"Pieces of eight! Pieces of eight!" it squawked, the pirates' name for their cherished silver coins.

Long John Silver greeted me warmly.

As I was deciding he wasn't the man Billy Bones had feared, I noticed a familiar figure sneaking out of the inn door.

"It's Black Dog!" I cried. "Stop him!"

Silver sent one of the guests chasing after Black Dog because he hadn't paid his bill. The guest never returned—Black Dog had run away.

Meanwhile, Silver chatted merrily. He seemed a most amiable fellow. A little later, we walked together to find the Squire and Dr. Livesey. When Silver left us, we all agreed he was the ideal man for our voyage to Treasure Island.

I loved the *Hispaniola*. Her tall masts were hung with a spider's web of ropes and rigging, and her broad sails spread like huge handkerchiefs in the wind. On board, all was sparkling clean and shipshape.

I was less pleased with Captain Smollett. He was a fine sailor, I was told. But he complained crossly about the crew that the Squire and Long John Silver had chosen.

He also grumbled that the voyage was meant to be secret—yet, every crew member knew they were sailing for treasure. He blamed the Squire for this, which made him very angry.

Dr. Livesey calmed things down. There were seven men we could trust, he said: himself, the Squire, the Captain, me, and four other honest men. We would sleep at the back of the ship, above

the storage of gunpowder and guns.

If the crew attacked us, we could defend our position like a little fort.

When Silver saw what was going on, he looked surprised. But when he heard it was the Captain's orders, he saluted and cried, "Aye, aye, sir!"

"What a good man he is," said Doctor Livesey.

"Maybe," replied the Captain, grimly.

The *Hispaniola* sailed smoothly across the Atlantic Ocean like a huge seabird. The weather was calm, and we made good progress. Our only problem was the ship's mate.

As the captain's right-hand man, the mate passed on orders to the crew and made sure they were obeyed. He was an officer, not one of the men.

But our mate, Mister Arrow, was always laughing and joking with the crew, who didn't respect him. Worse still, he had a

blurry look in his eye, staggered about, and spoke as if he had a stone in his mouth. In short, he seemed drunk.

As the days went by, the crew laughed at Arrow more and more. Captain Smollett was furious and refused to let him have any rum. But Arrow still managed to find a bottle somewhere.

Then, one dark night, when Arrow was on lookout duty, he disappeared.

Everyone said he had fallen overboard. Now that I know more about our crew, I think they were lying. Silver didn't trust Arrow. I reckon he'd given him rum and pushed him overboard.

Arrow was never seen again.

Why do I think Silver tipped Mister Arrow into the sea? Listen carefully, and I'll tell you.

We kept a barrel of apples on deck. One evening, toward the end of our voyage, I felt like some fresh fruit and went to get an apple. As there were only a few left at the bottom of the barrel, I climbed inside. There, rocked by the movement of the ship, I fell asleep.

I woke to hear voices. Silver was telling the crew horrible tales of Captain Flint, murder, and piracy. I curled up in the bottom of the barrel, praying no one wanted an apple. If they found me, they would surely kill me.

My blood ran cold. Long John Silver was the "seafaring man with one leg" who had terrified Billy Bones. He had

sailed with Captain Flint and knew all about the treasure map. Nearly all our crew were pirates!

Silver was planning to wait until we had dug up the treasure and got it safely on board the *Hispaniola*. Then he would murder me and all the honest men—and sail off with the treasure.

I was saved by a shout from the lookout: "Land ahoy!" We had reached Treasure Island.

CHAPTER 3

Going Ashore

Amid the excitement of seeing Treasure Island, I climbed out of the apple barrel unnoticed. I found Dr. Livesey and told him I had important news. Shortly afterward, he called me to the cabin to talk to himself, the Captain, and the Squire.

I told them what I had heard. Nearly all the crew were pirates, and Long John

Silver was their leader. They had sailed with us to steal the treasure—and they planned to murder every one of us.

It was a desperate situation. Nineteen pirates against us four, plus four loyal men: Hunter, Joyce, Gray, and Redruth. But we had one big advantage: We had the map marked with the spot where the treasure had been buried.

The Captain was worried that the pirates might try to get the map by attacking us. So, the next morning, he gave permission for the crew to go ashore. Thirteen went, rowing in two of the smaller boats.

I now did something very foolish. It was hot and stuffy on board, and the island looked green and exciting. Without telling anyone, I crept into one of the boats going ashore.

As soon as my boat ran into the sandy beach, I leaped out and ran off into the trees. I heard Silver calling after me, "Jim! Come back, Jim!" but I took no notice.

I ran until exhausted, then stopped and looked round. Wow! I had never been out of England before, and the sights, sounds, and scents of the island amazed me. There were trees rich with fruits and nuts, birds with bright feathers, and snakes slithering around my feet.

A rocky hill loomed over the whole island. Silver, who had been here before, had called it the Spyglass. I tried to remember Captain Flint's map and the place where the treasure was buried.

Just then, I heard voices coming toward me, and I dived for cover beneath some leafy bushes.

Moments later, two men came into sight. One was Long John Silver. The other was Tom, one of the few honest members of the crew. I listened carefully. Silver was trying to persuade him to join his gang, but Tom would have none of it.

Their conversation was interrupted by voices farther off. A shout of anger was followed by a long, horrible scream.

Tom turned pale when he heard the scream. "What's that?" he gasped.

Long John Silver remained as cool as a sea breeze. He said that the scream had come from Alan, another crew member who had refused to join his gang. Would Tom now change his mind?

"You've killed Alan," the man said grimly. "Kill me, too, if you can. I won't join you."

With that, he turned and walked off. Quick as a blink, Silver whipped his crutch from beneath his arm and flung it, point first, at Tom's back. It hit him between his shoulder blades, and he fell forward onto the ground.

Silver, knife drawn, was on him in a second. Two quick stabs, and it was all over.

The scene had been so cruel, so
bloodthirsty, that I fainted. When I came
to, I was terrified that I'd be Silver's next
victim. Heart pounding, I sprinted into
the woods.

Pausing beneath some spreading oaks
to catch my breath, I saw a figure leaping
between the trees. Surely this shaggy
beast wasn't a man? A bear, perhaps? Or
a monkey? Whatever it was, I was trapped
between it and the pirates behind me.

Running away won't do me any good,
I thought. I plucked up courage and
walked toward the strange creature.

He was a man! His hair
and beard hung down to
his shoulders, his skin was
baked black by the sun,
and his clothes were rags.
Hesitating, he edged forward
and knelt at my feet.

"Who are you?" I asked.

"My name is Ben Gunn," he answered
in a croaky voice, "and you are the first
person I have spoken to for three years."
He looked up anxiously. "Is that Flint's
ship I saw at anchor? Is there a man with
one leg on board?"

I told him Flint was dead, but many
of his men—including the one-legged

sailor—were the crew of the *Hispaniola.*

I asked Mr. Gunn how he knew about Captain Flint and Long John Silver. In reply, he told me his sad story.

Along with Long John Silver and Billy Bones, Ben Gunn had been a sailor on Captain Flint's ship. One day, the Captain had anchored off Treasure Island and gone ashore with his loot and six men. He returned alone, empty-handed, and without the six men. He'd killed them all after they'd helped him bury his treasure.

Later, Benn Gunn sailed back to Treasure Island on another ship. When he told two friends there was treasure ashore, all three went looking for it. They found nothing. Ben's friends were so angry that they left him on Treasure Island—and he had been there ever since.

Living alone for so long had made Ben a little odd. But he was also charming and friendly, and we were soon good friends.

"I can help you, Jim," he said with a pleasing smile.

"What do you mean?" I asked.

He winked at me and said, "Wait and see. But if I help you, you must help me."

"Fair enough," I replied. "What can I do for you?"

"Take me with you off this horrible island!" he cried. "Please!"

It seemed a good bargain. While we were talking, we heard gunfire. I now feared that my friends were in danger. We set off—I needed to join them as quickly as possible.

We were walking over some high rocks, when Ben Gunn stopped and pointed. I couldn't believe it. There, sticking up among the trees was a flagpole. On it, waving in the breeze, was a Union Jack!

CHAPTER 4

Battle Begins

After I had left the *Hispaniola,* my
friends on board grew restless. It was now
steaming hot, and they were worried what
the pirates were up to.

Dr. Livesey decided to take our last
small boat and go ashore. Hunter,
a loyal servant, agreed to go with him.
They would explore the island, look
for me, and spy on Silver and his gang.

The two men landed on the shore
and walked up a small hill. There, they
discovered a fort built by Captain Flint's
crew. A tall wooden fence surrounded
a stout log cabin. The entrance to the
cabin was open, and instead of windows
it had holes for firing shots. Dr. Livesey

thought the place was perfect for fighting off attackers.

He and Hunter went back to the *Hispaniola* and told the others what they had found. The Captain decided they should leave the ship and set up camp in the fort.

One man kept an eye on the pirates still on board, while the others went back and forth to the fort with supplies. However, on the last trip, no one was left to guard the pirates—who were then seen loading the *Hispaniola*'s cannon.

Boom! The cannon fired at the boat, which was carrying supplies to the fort. The Squire shot back with his musket.

Boom! The cannon fired again.

This was the gunfire I had heard when I was with Ben Gunn.

The cannonballs hit the sea near the boat. Since it was very full, the waves washed over its sides, and it sank. My friends snatched what supplies they could and waded ashore.

Meanwhile, on the island, Silver and his pirates heard the cannon's roar. They ran down to the beach and saw the Doctor leading the others toward the fort.

We now fought our first battle. One of our men, Redruth, was shot dead, but the others climbed the fence and got safely inside the fort. Several pirates were hit by our shots, so there were fewer of them now.

The battle had stopped by the time I reached the fort. I said goodbye to Ben Gunn, scrambled over the fence, and ran into the cabin. Everyone was relieved to see me, but their faces were deadly serious.

There we were, thousands of miles from home, on a desert island with food for just ten days, surrounded by murderous pirates.

Things looked very grim.

When I was safe inside the cabin, I told the others about Ben Gunn. He said he'd help us if we needed him. Only later did we understand what he meant.

I also mentioned that I'd seen the pirate camp. Then, they had been gathered around a roaring fire, singing, arguing, and drinking rum. Though they were twice our numbers, they wouldn't be much good at fighting for a while.

Captain Smollett kept our spirits up. He gave us all a position and a job to do. Mine was to carry loaded guns to the men shooting out through the round holes—"loopholes" the Captain called them.

Early the next morning, we had a surprise visit. Long John Silver and a man carrying a white flag on a stick approached the fort. Silver wanted to make a deal.

"If you hand over the map showing where the treasure is," he said, "we'll split the money between us. Then, we'll all sail home together. If that worries you, stay here with your half of the treasure. I'll send a ship to pick you up. That's a promise."

"Your promises," said the Captain angrily, "are not worth a bucket of seawater! Leave us!"

We had all left our positions while the Captain was talking with Silver. After he had gone, the Captain was furious. "To your positions!" he roared.

Three hours later, the attack began. The enemy swarmed up the fence like monkeys. We fired back through the loopholes and the cabin was soon full of smoke.

Our shooting was accurate, but the pirates were brave and determined. Four of them got over the fence and ran toward the cabin. One of them seized Hunter's gun and knocked him out. Another shot Joyce through the head.

"Attack!" commanded the Captain.

"Outside with cutlasses!"

We each grabbed a curved sword and ran into the open space between the cabin and the fence. I came face-to-face with Anderson, one of the pirate leaders. He yelled  and swung his sword at me. As I dodged, I tripped and rolled over in the sand.

By the time I got up, the pirates were fleeing back over the fence. We had won!

We had slain six pirates, leaving just eight. But victory had its price. Joyce was dead, and the Captain was very badly wounded. That left just five of us: the Squire, the Doctor, Hunter, Gray, and myself, the cabin boy.

After the attack, we were unable to relax in case the pirates returned. What could we do? We knew where the treasure was, but we didn't dare go and get it.

Dr. Livesey decided to go and talk with Benn Gun, and he went to meet him. I had a secret plan of my own.

The most important thing in the whole adventure was the *Hispaniola*. She had brought us here, and only she could take us home again. But the ship was now in the hands of the pirates.

My idea was to sail out to her, cut her anchor rope, and let her drift onto the shore. The pirates would then have no way of leaving—even if they found the treasure.

I remembered Ben Gunn telling me about a little boat he had made

from goat skin stretched over a wooden
frame. He called it a "coracle," and I
knew where it was hidden …

That evening, I took some sea biscuits
and a pair of pistols, and sneaked out
of the fort. I soon found the coracle
and carried it down to the sea. The
Hispaniola was riding at anchor only
a short distance away.

CHAPTER 5

My Sea Adventure

I waited until dark, then slipped the coracle into the water. It wobbled crazily,

 nearly tipping me into the sea. But after a time, it settled down, and I started to paddle.

I now had another problem. Because the coracle was round, my paddling made it spin in circles! Luckily, the tide was flowing toward the ship, and I finally got close enough to grab the thick anchor rope. Opening my knife with my teeth, I began to cut through it.

From the open cabin window above me, I heard two angry voices.

I recognized one as Israel Hands, Captain Flint's gunner. The other belonged to a man I'd seen in a red nightcap. By the sound of their shouting and swearing, they were both drunk.

Silver had left these two men to look after the *Hispaniola* while the other pirates were ashore. Huh! I thought. They're not doing a very good job!

With a final effort, I sliced through the last strands of rope. Immediately, the *Hispaniola* swung around in the current. The ship's heavy bows swept toward my little coracle. If we collided, it would be smashed to pieces, and I would surely drown.

I fought like a fiend to save my little craft. Inch by inch, I pushed it along the hull to the back—or "stern"—of the *Hispaniola*. In the starlight, I spied a rope hanging down from above the cabin from where the voices were coming.

As you know, I sometimes act without thinking. That's what I did now. For some reason, seeing the rope, I grabbed hold of it. Up I went, hand over hand, to see what was going on in the cabin.

One glance was enough. Israel Hands and the red nightcap man were wrestling furiously. Each man had a hand on the other's throat. It looked like a fight to the death.

I dropped back down into the coracle and drifted slowly away from the *Hispaniola*. On the beach to my left, I

could see the pirates gathered around
their bonfire. Sparks flew high into the
night sky, and the sound of singing
floated across the calm, dark sea:

"Fifteen men on the dead man's chest—
Yo-ho-ho, and a bottle of rum!"

The words reminded me of my
mother and the happy times we had
spent together at the Admiral Benbow.
How I longed to be back there!

Lulled by the rocking of my little boat, I fell into a deep sleep. When I awoke, it was broad daylight. I looked around.

During the night, I had drifted to a part of the island I didn't know. To my dismay, a strong current was pulling me farther from the shore. The sea was getting rougher, too. Waves splashed over the sides of the coracle, and I had to stop paddling to bail out the water. I was terrified the craft would sink.

I looked up. Impossible! Only a short distance away, I saw the *Hispaniola* drifting out of control. I paddled furiously toward her, and managed to grab a rope and pull myself aboard just as the coracle sank.

I found the two seamen flat out on the deck. The red nightcap man was dead; Israel Hands looked badly wounded.

"Right," I said, "I'm the captain of this ship now. If you tell me how to sail her, Mr. Hands, I'll tend your wounds and bring you something to drink."

Hands agreed, and I soon had the *Hispaniola* under control. But the pirate was not as ill as he looked. Worse, I knew he had a knife hidden inside his jacket.

We guided the *Hispaniola* into a cove known as the North Anchorage. I planned to steer her safely aground on soft sand.

I was concentrating so hard, I didn't notice Hands standing up. Suddenly, he was lurching toward me. In his right hand, he held a gleaming knife.

I grasped one of my pistols and fired. There was a dull click. The gunpowder was damp, and the gun didn't go off.

At that moment, the *Hispaniola* struck a sandbank. She tipped to one side, throwing Hands and myself to the deck. I recovered quickly and climbed up the rigging beside the mast.

Slowly and painfully, Hands came after me, holding the knife between his teeth. I quickly reloaded my guns with dry powder.

When the pirate was a few feet below

me, I pointed my pistols at him.

"Not another step, Mr. Hands," I cried.

I'm not sure what happened next.
Hands whipped the knife from his mouth
and flung it at me. It hit my shoulder,
pinning me to the mast. At the same time,
I fired both pistols. The guns fell out of
my hands and tumbled, together with
Israel Hands, into the clear blue sea.

Hands's knife had nailed me to the mast by my jacket. Luckily, the blade had only grazed my shoulder. I set myself free and cut down the mainsail, so that the vessel wouldn't move with the wind. I then tidied up the rest of the ship. By early evening, the *Hispaniola* was secure and in good order.

I was eager to tell my friends what I had done. Using Spyglass Hill to discover my position, I worked out that the fort was quite near. I decided to go there immediately.

I dived off the ship and swam ashore. Though it was dark by the time I got there, the fort was easy to find. That's strange, I thought, as I climbed the fence. No one on guard? The Captain will be furious.

I tiptoed through the door and listened to the men's snores. I smiled.

Instead of waking them, I'd sleep on the floor—they'd get such a surprise finding me there in the morning!

But the surprise was all mine. The silence of the night was suddenly broken by a harsh cry: "Pieces of eight! Piece of eight!"

It was Long John Silver's parrot. The pirates had captured the fort!

CHAPTER 6

Treasure

When I realized I was in a nest of pirates, I dashed for the door. A strong arm grabbed me and brought me back.

The villains fingered their daggers and gave me murderous looks. They wanted to kill me! "Let me live," I argued, "and I'll defend you in the law courts back in England." Five of the men sneered, saying that I couldn't be trusted.

But not Long John Silver. He said he'd save my life now, if I saved his in England.

At this, the men muttered angrily. They handed Silver a Black Spot warning, written on a page torn from a Bible: He was no longer their leader.

"Not your leader?" he laughed. "So,

you don't want this?" From his pocket, he
pulled Billy Bones's map showing where
the treasure was buried.

We were astonished! How had Silver
found the map, we asked.

He grinned and said that Dr. Livesey
had given it to him. The two of them
had come to a kind of agreement. I also
learned the pirates were in the fort because
my friends had abandoned it when they
discovered the *Hispaniola* was missing.

I was now utterly confused.

I was even more confused when Dr. Livesey appeared at the fort. He had come, he said, to treat the wounded pirates. It was his duty as a doctor to heal the sick and injured, whoever they were.

This was very brave of him. I feared that the pirates, like savage dogs, might turn on him at any moment. I asked Silver if I might speak to the Doctor in private.

He agreed, if I gave him my word that I would not try to escape.

I promised.

At first, the Doctor was angry with me for running away and getting captured by Silver. But he soon changed. He was delighted when I told him how I had taken the *Hispaniola* from the pirates and hidden it in the North Anchorage. I had saved the honest men yet again!

"So, come on!" he urged. "Jump over the fence with me, and leave these dreadful people!"

"I'd love to," I said, "but I have given my word. If I broke my promise, I'd be no better than a pirate, would I?"

The Doctor nodded sadly and departed. Once again, I was alone and at the mercy of Long John Silver.

After the Doctor left, we left to find the treasure. Silver, map in hand, led the way. I was attached to him by a rope, like a dog on a leash. The other five pirates trailed along behind.

At first, we trudged slowly through the marshy jungle. The ground was drier on the slopes of Spyglass Hill, where Flint's treasure lay, and Silver hobbled quicker. He was eager to reach his goal.

In a clearing, we found the skeleton of one of the pirates Captain Flint had killed. It was propped up against a tree, its arms pointing toward the treasure.

The sight gave the pirates the jitters. As they were wondering whether Flint's ghost was nearby, a weird voice began singing his old song:

"Fifteen men on the dead man's chest—
Yo-ho-ho, and a bottle of rum!"

The pirates were scared out of their wits, until Silver cried, "It's Ben Gunn; the old fool marooned here. Nobody minds Ben Gunn!"

The pirates agreed. Much relieved, they hurried on toward the long-awaited treasure trove.

"Hurrah!" they yelled, as they reached the spot marked with an X on the map. "We're rich …"

They stopped. Before them lay a deep pit, a deep, *empty* pit.

The treasure had gone.

In the pit lay a broken shovel and some empty boxes. Before we had arrived, someone had dug up Flint's treasure and carried it off.

The five pirates were furious and swore at Silver. George Merry, the angriest of them, said the one-legged seaman had swindled them. "We'll kill you, Silver," he yelled, "and that wretched boy too!"

At that moment, there was a crackle of gunfire from the bushes nearby. Merry tumbled over headlong into the pit, another one of his mates collapsed to the ground, the other three ran for their lives.

Then, all at once, Dr. Livesey, Gray, and Ben Gunn came out of hiding, guns smoking. Long John Silver—the crafty devil!—reminded the Doctor that he had

saved my life. He was one of the Squire's team now, he said.

The Doctor explained it all to me. During his three years on the island, Ben Gunn had dug up the treasure and moved it to a secret cave high on Spyglass Hill. He then explained this to Dr. Livesey. That's why the Doctor had been happy to give Billy Bones's map to Silver—the X no longer marked the spot where Flint's treasure was hidden.

The treasure of Treasure Island—seven
hundred thousand pounds—was ours!

*

The rest of my tale is swiftly told. Ben
Gunn showed us the cave in which he'd
hidden Flint's treasure. The Squire and
the Captain were keeping guard.

We found the *Hispaniola* safe and
sound in the North Anchorage. Carefully,
we carried on board the bars of gold and
bags of precious coins. When we were
ready to leave, we had to decide what to
do with the pirates.

Long John Silver and Ben Gunn
could come with us. We chose to leave
behind the three men who had run away.
To help them in their lonely life, we left
them gunpowder, food, medicine, tools,
clothes, tobacco, and a few other useful
bits and pieces.

As we were sailing away, they stood
on the shore gesturing to us, begging us
to take them with us. What could we do?
Back in England, they would be hanged
for piracy. We sailed on.

I have one more thing to report.
After sailing for some time, we stopped in
South America to stock up on supplies.
After returning to the ship, we found that
Long John Silver had stolen a sack of gold
coins and disappeared. We were all glad
to be rid of him.

At last, as I entered the Admiral Benbow Inn and threw myself into my mother's arms, my Treasure Island adventure was finally over.